CW00430738

British Library Cataloguing in Publication Data

Todd, H.E.
   The sleeping policeman.
   I. Title   II. Biro, Val
823′.914[J]   PZ7

   ISBN 0-340-41299-2

Text copyright © H. E. Todd 1988
Illustrations copyright © Val Biro 1988

First published 1988

Published by Hodder and Stoughton Children's Books,
a division of Hodder and Stoughton Ltd,
Mill Road, Dunton Green, Sevenoaks, Kent TN13 2YJ

Printed in Great Britain by Cambus Litho,
East Kilbride

All rights reserved

THE SLEEPING POLICEMAN

Story by
H. E. TODD

Pictures by
VAL BIRO

HODDER AND STOUGHTON
LONDON SYDNEY AUCKLAND TORONTO

Do you know what a 'sleeping policeman' is? It is the name often given to those ramps sometimes built across private roads to stop cars from being driven too fast. After all, the ramps *are* lying down as if asleep, and *do* control the traffic like a policeman.

A sleeping policeman like that was built across the drive leading to the school. Very smart it was, too, with yellow and black stripes, and it certainly slowed down parents driving their children to school in a last-minute rush.

Bobby Brewster thought that it was such a clever sleeping policeman, to be able to control traffic in its sleep, that it deserved to be given a proper name. He and his friends decided to call the sleeping policeman Police Constable Tufftummy, because he was strong enough to allow cars to drive over him. And on their way to and from school every day they danced by him singing:

P.C.   P.C.

   TUFF   TUFF

      TUMMY   TUMMY

Then, one evening when Bobby was returning home from school all by himself, later than usual, a funny thing happened. He heard the sound of snoring – and it came from the sleeping policeman!

Then an even funnier thing happened. The sleeping policeman uncovered his face, sat up, and said, 'Good evening, young man.'

Bobby stood tongue-tied.

'I am Police Constable Tufftummy,' announced the sleeping policeman, and Bobby realised that he must have heard the children singing his name.

Then he stood up, all three metres of him, dressed in a smart yellow and black striped tracksuit.

'I thought you were supposed to be a *sleeping* policeman,' said Bobby.

'I am during school hours,' was the reply, 'but every evening I do my exercises.'

'Exercises?'

'Yes,' said P.C. Tufftummy. And to prove it he got down on his hands and knees and did five press-ups! Then he added: 'After that I go jogging.'

'Jogging?' cried Bobby.

'It's part of my training,' said P.C. Tufftummy, 'but only when no one is about. During the day I'm a sleeping policeman and allow cars to drive over me.'

'It must be very uncomfortable,' said Bobby.

P.C. Tufftummy then stood on his head – all three metres of him – and replied (upside down): 'It was at first but' (right side up) 'now I'm used to it.' Then he explained: 'It slows down traffic and strengthens my stomach muscles at the same time.'

He performed a perfect double somersault – all three metres of him – and added: 'As I said, it's all part of my training.'

'What are you training for?' asked Bobby.

'The Super Strong Man of the Year contest on the television,' was the reply. 'But keep it a secret. I don't want crowds interfering with my training. And be sure to ask your friends to watch the programme on Thursday at 8 p.m. I should like to feel that I have plenty of support.'

'I most certainly will,' promised Bobby.

'Come on, now, let's jog,' said P.C. Tufftummy, and they jogged together to the end of the drive, where the constable turned round and jogged back towards the school and Bobby jogged on homewards.

On the following morning Bobby told his friends to be sure to look in on Thursday, but he couldn't explain why, because it was a secret. He himself could hardly wait for Thursday to come and the programme to start.

And what an exciting broadcast it turned out to be – a contest between six huge, strong men, each the strongest in his own district.

They were announced in turn:

Burly Bill Baxter from Barnstaple.

Daring Dai Davis from Dolgellau.

Angus McTavish, the Terror from Tighnabruach.

Mike O'Malley, the mighty Midget from Magherafelt.

Henry Hickinbottom, the Hulk from Heckmondwike.

And last, but by no means least, Police Constable Tufftummy – all three metres of him – in his smart yellow and black striped tracksuit.

Then the contest started.
First they all lifted enormous, heavy weights.

Then they bent strong iron bars.

Then they loaded lorries with huge sacks in record times.

Then they pushed their lorries one-handed along a track.

The lead changed after each event, and when the last contest was due there was very little to choose between the contestants. Excitement was at fever pitch.

For the final test they were allowed to display their own chosen feat of strength.

Bill Baxter pulled a bus along with his teeth.

Dai Davis smashed bricks with his bare hands.

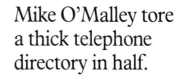

Mike O'Malley tore a thick telephone directory in half.

Angus McTavish tossed a huge caber in the air and caught it.

Henry Hickinbottom turned a loaded van over on its side.

Then came Police Constable Tufftummy – all three metres of him. Can you guess what he did? He lay down on the track and allowed two cars, a van and a minibus full of passengers to ride over him, a feat that none of the other competitors could ever have attempted. After all, that was what he had been doing on the school drive as a sleeping policeman, wasn't it?

Needless to say, he was given maximum points and, amidst great applause, Police Constable Tufftummy was declared to be THE SUPER STRONG MAN OF THE YEAR. Then, as the band played the national anthem, he stood on a rostrum – all three metres of him – and a gold medal on a gold ribbon was hung around his neck by Princess Someone-or-other, who had to borrow a ladder to reach.

Bobby Brewster was very proud of his friend.

At school on the following morning the children and teachers who had watched the programme could talk about nothing else. They all said how amazing it was that the winner of the contest had exactly the same name as they had chosen for the sleeping policeman across the school drive. They never guessed for one moment that they were one and the same person. Bobby Brewster knew differently, but he didn't say anything because it was a secret.

One other funny thing happened. On the spot where the medal had been hung a gold circle appeared on one of the sleeping policeman's black stripes. On dark nights it shone like a cat's eye, which proved to be very useful for slowing down cars at crowded events in the school hall. But no one could imagine how it got there – except Bobby Brewster that is.

The children still dance by the sleeping policeman every day and they sing:

P.C.   P.C.

     TUFF   TUFF

         TUMMY   TUMMY

but since then he has slept soundly day and night. Perhaps he put so much effort into winning the Super Strong Man of the Year contest that he completely wore himself out and is relieved to be a sleeping policeman all the time.

I wonder if he will ever wake up again.

I have my doubts.